I WITNESSED
THE BHOPAL GAS TRAGEDY

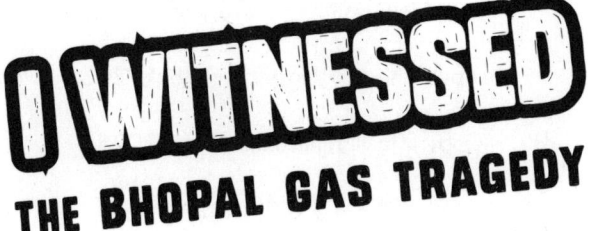
THE BHOPAL GAS TRAGEDY

JOHN SMITH-SREEN

JUGGERNAUT BOOKS
C-I-128, First Floor, Sangam Vihar, Near Holi Chowk,
New Delhi 110080, India

First published by Juggernaut Books 2025

Copyright © John Smith-Sreen 2025

10 9 8 7 6 5 4 3 2 1

P-ISBN: 9789353456535
E-ISBN: 9789353459697

The views and opinions expressed in this book are the author's own. The facts contained herein were reported to be true as on the date of publication by the author to the publishers of the book, and the publishers are not in any way liable for their accuracy or veracity.

This book contains descriptions of real-life disasters and loss of life. Reader discretion is advised.

All rights reserved. No part of this publication may be reproduced, transmitted or stored in a retrieval system in any form or by any means without the written permission of the publisher.

Typeset in Futura Std by R. Ajith Kumar, Noida

Printed at Thomson Press India Ltd

*To the Sreens and the Sonis who welcomed
me to India as one of their own and
shared with me so many inspirational stories
that needed to be told.*

CONTENTS

1. The Night That Became a Nightmare   1
2. When the Air Became a Killer   13
3. The Train That Stopped   23
4. Siren's Call   39
5. When the Dead Filled the Streets   53
6. In the Safe House   65
7. Stay or Leave?   79
8. Hospital Without Cures   91
9. A New Friendship   105
10. Recalling the Tragedy   115

Why We Must Remember   122

1

THE NIGHT THAT BECAME A NIGHTMARE

Vikram Soni walked home through the dark streets of Bhopal. The darkness didn't bother him – he knew every bend and shortcut here like the back of his hand. Besides, the quiet gave him space to think about things other than school.

Earlier that night, he and his friends had sneaked out to the new community centre on top of the hill. Normally, they met there for their study group, but tonight was different. His parents had left town just after sunset, leaving him in charge of his little brother, Suresh.

They wouldn't be back until the next evening. For twenty-four whole hours, Vikram was his own man. It was the perfect excuse to bend a few rules.

After dinner, with Suresh fast asleep, Vikram had slipped out and made the short climb to the centre, where his friends were already waiting. The chowkidar, a kind old man who knew them well, had waved them in as always.

'Just one tube light,' the chowkidar reminded them as he did always, wagging his finger. 'No air conditioner!'

Vikram and his friends didn't mind. They came to the community centre for the company – and the chance to wrestle with tough subjects like math and science. They had just started Class 11 and everyone was stressing them out about university and exams. Chemistry was Vikram's favourite subject. He loved the way elements could join to make something new, something useful. Maybe one day, he thought, he'd be a chemical engineer. Or was that too boring?

Still, they didn't study all the time. Between equations, they talked about cricket, cheered for Team India and sometimes gossiped about the Union Carbide plant nearby.

Union Carbide was part of Bhopal's skyline. Everyone knew it made pesticides for farmers. Lately, though, the newspapers had been running stories about pollution and 'dangerous chemicals'.

One journalist had written: 'Wake up, people of Bhopal – you are on the edge of a volcano.' The boys had laughed and called out those words to each other like a joke. But for Vikram, it wasn't so funny. What did that journalist know that others didn't? There had been rumours of leaks before …

When the mood turned serious, they speculated: what if there really was a leak? What would we do?

Vikram was the only one who could remember both dangerous chemicals: cyanide and methyl isocyanate – MIC for short. Both could kill.

But his mind was far from serious thoughts as he strolled home. It felt thrilling to be out alone at night, the cool air on his face making him feel grown-up – free as a bird. But the rush was edged with guilt. Suresh was still at home, asleep, all alone.

Brrrrrring!

A warning alarm suddenly rang out across the neighbourhood – sharp and loud. Then, just as suddenly, it stopped.

Dogs started barking. Woof-woof-woof! Then they began howling.

Vikram's steps quickened. Something about that alarm made his stomach tighten into a knot.

His house lay between the Union Carbide plant and the Upper Lake, in an older neighbourhood of narrow, crowded streets. His mind went to Suresh, all alone at home. His parents would be furious if they knew.

'I should never have left him alone,' Vikram muttered. He broke into a sprint. Thud-thud-thud! His sandals slapped against the road.

As he passed the plant, he heard shouting inside the compound. He slowed, his breath puffing in the cool night air, and looked up at the looming structure.

The front gate banged open – CLANG! – and a flood of workers came spilling out.

'Run!' one man yelled.

'Why?' Vikram called back.

'Just run!' the man shouted without stopping.

More workers rushed past him, their faces twisted in fear.

That was enough for Vikram. If they were running, he was running.

He darted down side streets towards home, the shouts fading behind him. His mind spun – something was wrong at the plant. But what?

By the time his pace slowed, he told himself it would be contained quickly. Surely it couldn't be that bad.

He was wrong. Very wrong.

Vikram had just witnessed the beginning of one of the worst industrial disasters the world would ever know: the Bhopal Gas Tragedy.

2

WHEN THE AIR BECAME A KILLER

By the time Vikram burst through his front door, he was gasping for breath. His chest felt tight, like he couldn't get enough air. His eyes itched and a dry cough scraped at his throat.

First thing: Suresh. He dashed into the bedroom and found the five-year-old curled up under the blanket, breathing softly.

Phew.

Vikram leaned against the door frame, telling himself he had overreacted. Maybe the workers at the plant had panicked over nothing. Still, he splashed water on his face in the bathroom.

The sight of the boy in the mirror made him pause. Red, bloodshot eyes stared back at him.

You look terrible, he told his reflection. *Don't you dare fall sick now – you've got so much studying to do.*

In the first-aid box, he rummaged through medicines for paracetamol. His cough was sharper now, and his tongue felt dry.

Then he became aware – outside, the dogs were still barking. Not just barking – howling, whining, frantic.

Vikram stepped onto the veranda.

WHAM! An awful stench hit him. It was like a thousand cabbages boiling in a thousand kitchens all at once. He gagged, his eyes watering.

Somewhere down the lane, shouting echoed. Then an old man staggered into view, clutching his chest. He stumbled, fell hard onto the pavement – THUD! – and lay still.

Vikram's heart lurched. This wasn't just a problem at the plant. It was here, in his street.

He bolted inside. 'Suresh! Wake up!'

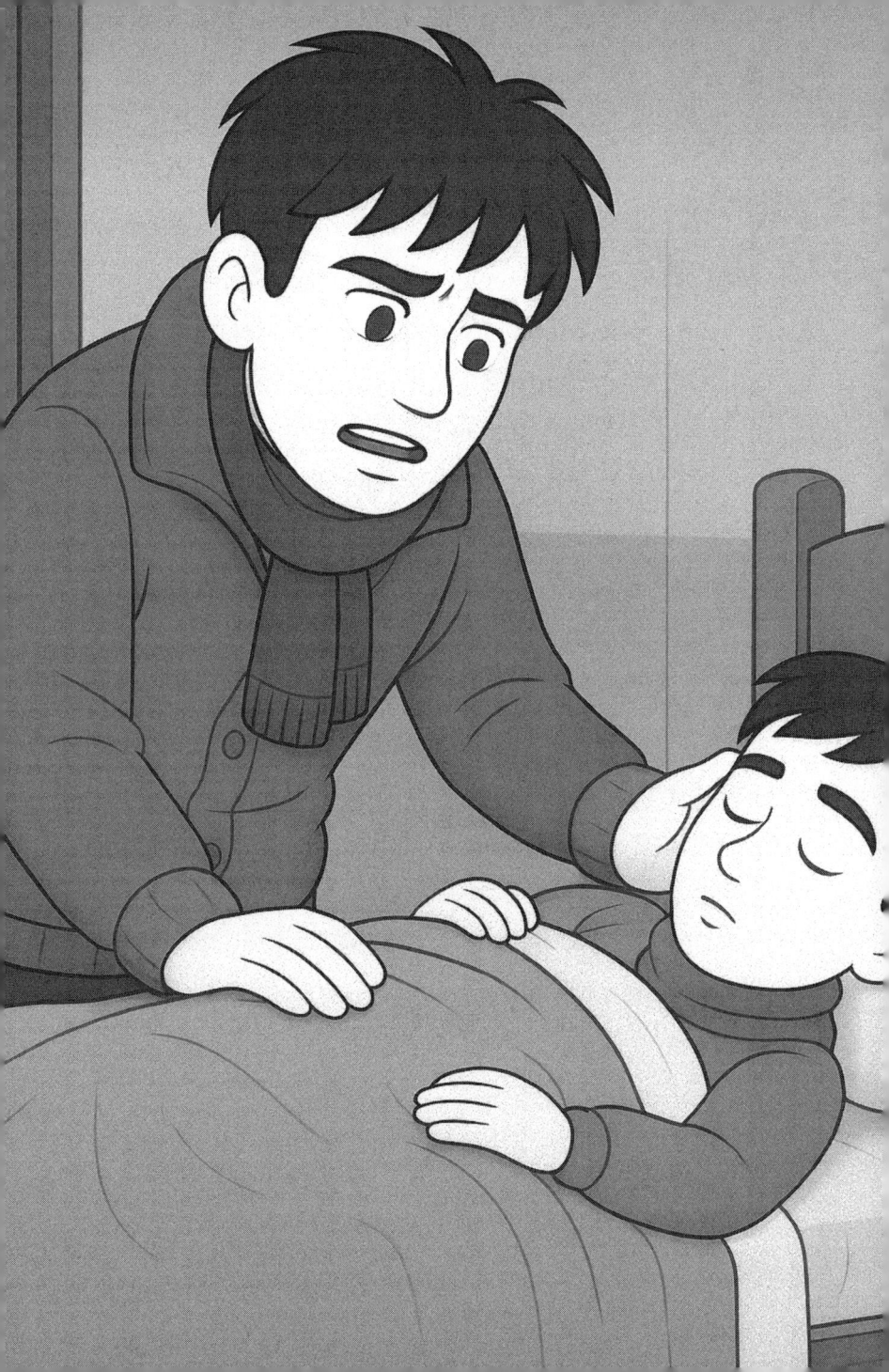

'Mmm ... why?' Suresh mumbled, rubbing his eyes.

'I'm sorry, but we can't stay here. Something's happened at the Union Carbide plant.'

That got Suresh's attention. His eyes widened, though he didn't fully understand.

'Quick – find some of Mama's dupattas!' Vikram said urgently.

'What for?'

'To cover our faces,' Vikram replied. 'And we're heading to the new community centre. They sealed the windows for the air conditioning – it's higher up, and safer from the gas.'

From his science lessons, he remembered: gas is heavier than oxygen. You move higher to escape it. And if you have to breathe, you breathe through something wet.

He swallowed hard. Each breath could be their last.

While Suresh hunted for dupattas, Vikram soaked a handkerchief and tied it around

his own nose and mouth. The damp cloth felt clammy but safe.

Then he was out of the door again, pounding on his neighbours' doors. BANG-BANG-BANG!

'Wake up! Wake up! There's gas! There's gas!'

Faces peered out – confused, frightened. Some homes were already lit; others still dark.

'Tell your neighbours!' Vikram shouted. 'Go to the community centre! Wear a mask – wet it with water! It will protect you!'

Some people nodded, pulling children from beds. Others hesitated, not sure whether to believe him. But the smell was everywhere now, and the coughing had begun.

Vikram dashed back inside to find Suresh clutching their mother's dupattas. 'Here!' Suresh said, breathless.

Vikram quickly wet them at the kitchen sink, tying one over Suresh's nose and mouth. The

younger boy's eyes were huge, but he didn't complain.

They stepped out into the street together. The air was heavy and bitter. All around them, doors banged open, voices called out and bare feet slapped against the pavement.

A woman coughed so hard she doubled over. A man carried a child who was limp in his arms.

'Come on!' Vikram urged Suresh, gripping his hand. 'Every second counts.'

The two boys moved quickly towards the hill, the smell of cabbages and the sound of coughing following them into the night.

3
THE TRAIN THAT STOPPED

'Oh, Kanta, come sit next to me!' Sushma called out, patting the seat beside her. Her eyes sparkled with excitement.

The coolie had just finished loading their luggage, and Papa had tipped him generously. The man's face split into a grin. Papa always did that – generous to anyone connected with the railways. After all, he'd worked in the railway system for years, and the people in it felt like family.

Raising two girls alone since their mother's death hadn't been easy. At times, the responsibility pressed down on him so heavily it was hard to breathe. And then there was Sushma – his lively, pretty little firecracker – who knew exactly how to test his limits. Well, not so little anymore. She was on the verge of becoming a young woman, about to begin preparing for her Class 10 exams. Over the past year, it felt as if every conversation between them had turned into a challenge.

'What will you wear for the sangeet, Kanta?' Sushma asked, and didn't wait for an answer. 'I'll wear the green salwar kameez ... no, maybe my deep blue sari, for the wedding itself. Or should I wear the yellow salwar with the green piping? Green looks good on me, don't you think? I definitely want to wear a sari. Papa will let me this time, right?'

Kanta, at five, didn't talk much. She just smiled and tilted her head, the way she always did when her sister went on and on.

'Good, it's settled – the yellow salwar!' Sushma declared. Then she frowned. 'But the green one's so pretty ...'

Kanta thought privately, 'She'll probably end up wearing the maroon one,' and grinned to herself.

'What? What's so funny?' Sushma demanded. But before Kanta could say a word, she was off again. 'Isn't it wonderful? We have half the compartments in this sleeper car!'

The overnight train was full of Sharmas from Delhi, all headed to Bhopal for the wedding. Weddings meant singing, dancing, endless food – and all the cousins together.

Clang-clang! Whoo-hoo! The train jolted forward, Delhi slipping away as the scenery turned into green and gold fields. Water buffalo stood knee-deep in ponds, chewing grass lazily. Families sat on charpais in the fading light, talking about the day.

By nightfall, Papa told them to spread their sheets and go to bed. 'Papa, I don't want to sleep so early,' Sushma had said. 'Me too, me too,' said Kanta excitedly. 'Let's stay up all

night.' But Papa had hushed them sternly. 'Don't worry,' Sushma whispered to Kanta. 'He'll be asleep in no time, and we can do what we want. He always spoils our fun.'

The train rattled on through the heart of India – towards Madhya Pradesh, towards Bhopal.

At dawn, it screeched to a halt. Not unusual – trains often stopped to let others pass. But this time, they weren't at a station. Just fields stretching out forever.

Passengers peered out of windows. 'Why have we stopped?' someone called. Railway staff hurried through the aisles, but no one explained. Minutes dragged into hours. People argued with the staff. Papa moved between compartments, keeping the family calm.

Sushma tugged at him. 'Papa, what's happening?'

'I'll tell you when I know,' he snapped. 'Now keep quiet.'

Her mouth dropped open in outrage. Papa was so unreasonable. Do this. Do that. All the time.

Rumours swirled – broken tracks, engine trouble, other trains taking priority. Then whispers began: 'Something's happened … in Bhopal.' No one knew what, but unease spread like smoke.

'What do you think it is, Kanta?' Sushma whispered. 'We're going to miss the celebrations!'

Papa hushed them again. 'We wait for the conductor. No guessing.'

Then – thump-thump-thump – a line of police boots sounded in the corridor. Leading them was their uncle, a senior officer in Bhopal.

'Uncle?' Sushma blinked. 'What's he doing here? He should be at home, getting ready for the wedding!'

Papa stepped aside with him. They spoke in low voices – Papa nodding, then shaking his

head sharply, then gripping his brother-in-law's shoulder. When Papa turned back, his face was pale.

'Pack your things. We're going with your uncle.'

Even Sushma fell silent for a moment.

Papa went to tell the rest of the Sharmas. When he came back, he said only, 'It's serious. We don't know everything yet. The police will take us into Bhopal and keep us safe.'

Sushma bristled. She hated when Papa kept things from her.

There were no coolies here, in the middle of nowhere. They'd have to carry their own luggage. Sushma complained until a kind officer took her suitcase — and Kanta's too.

Climbing down from the carriage onto sharp stones, they made their way along the narrow bund of a rice paddy. 'Careful,' Papa warned, helping the girls balance.

By the time they reached the police van, Sushma's mood had sunk to a grumble. The ride into Bhopal was bumpy, the air hot and dusty.

'Pipe down,' Papa told her. 'Your uncle will take care of us.'

But Sushma crossed her arms and stared out of the window, not convinced.

4

SIREN'S CALL

The neighbourhood was wide awake now – shouts, coughs and cries filled the air. Doors banged open. Somewhere, a baby wailed. Vikram urged everyone he passed, 'Hurry! To the community centre! Wear a mask! Tell your neighbours!'

Suresh had done exactly as told. The wet dupattas were serving the boys well as masks. Suresh had even packed extra cloths, bottles of water and a small packet of snacks.

'You did good, Suresh,' Vikram said, surprised and proud.

Suresh grinned despite the tension in the air.

'Let's go.' Vikram hoisted his little brother onto his shoulders and took off at a jog. His voice rang out in the darkness, 'Please, there is gas! Come to the community centre! Wear a mask!'

Some neighbours rushed to join them. Others looked confused, calling, 'What gas? Who are you, boy?'

The coughing was everywhere now. People bent double, retching by the roadside. Vikram's chest tightened – not just from the run, but from fear. Every step brought new horror: a man lying motionless, a woman with white foam at her mouth, a child lying over a still body.

Suresh whimpered and buried his face in Vikram's shoulder. The road was a nightmare.

From a dark doorway, a shadow leapt – snatching the dupatta right off Suresh's face.

'Hey!' Vikram shouted, but the thief was gone in seconds, running into a side lane, cloth pressed to his own face.

Vikram set Suresh down, dug out another

dupatta from the bag, wet it and tied it firmly over his brother's mouth and nose. 'Good thing you packed lots,' he said, trying to joke.

Around the corner came six figures, stumbling, eyes streaming. Panic was written all over their faces.

'Quick – follow us!' Vikram shouted, trying to sound braver than he felt. They didn't hesitate.

Up the hill they ran until the community centre came into view. The chowkidar stepped out, puzzled.

'What's all this noise?' he asked.

'Gas leak! Open the gate – quickly!'

He recognized Vikram and didn't argue. The heavy gate swung open. Moments later, the front door followed. Vikram, Suresh and the group of six rushed in, soon followed by dozens more.

Vikram set Suresh on top of the study table. Vikram knew keeping him off the floor was safer – the gas was heavier than air. Every extra bit of height mattered, especially for a child's smaller lungs.

'Stay here,' he said to the little boy sternly. Suresh nodded, dazed and in shock.

One of the new arrivals grabbed Vikram's arm. 'What should we do?'

'I'm just a kid!'

'You brought us here – you must know something!' the man rasped between coughs.

Something clicked inside Vikram. 'Seal the place! Keep the front door shut – check all the windows!'

The chowkidar took the door. Vikram sprinted from room to room – windows tightly shut, thank goodness – handing out spare dupattas to anyone without protection.

The large hall was filling fast – over a hundred people now. Red eyes. Harsh, hacking coughs. People collapsed onto the floor.

From across the room – cough! cough! cough! – an old man on a charpai was struggling for air. Vikram rushed over.

The man was a doctor and an old friend of his parents. 'You're doing well, Vikram,' he gasped. 'Keep them away from the gas. Wash faces. Keep mouths and noses covered. Don't let them leave. I wish I was well enough to help.' Vikram nodded, blinking fast.

The chowkidar dragged in his charpai for an old woman gasping for breath. Vikram bathed her face with water, but within minutes, her coughing stopped, replaced by the wails of her daughter.

Vikram's eyes stung with more than gas. He had never seen anyone die in front of him. He turned away, blinking hard. Everything in his body felt heavy. 'I'm not a grown-up, I don't know anything,' he whispered to no one.

He turned to look at the doctor. The old man was slumped on the charpai. His eyes stared at nothing.

Vikram's stomach dropped. 'Doctor Sahib …?' No answer. He swallowed hard. But there was

no time to stop. 'Keep your masks on! Sit if you can! Stay calm!' he called out. 'Bhaiya, where are you going? Come here!' Suresh's voice cracked as he tried to scramble down from the table.

'Stay where you are!' Vikram shouted, in a tone sharper than he meant.

'I'm scared!' Suresh cried. His eyes darted around the room – rows of sick people groaning, coughing, gasping for breath. The smell of medicine and sweat hung in the air. And outside … those awful scenes on the road. For a five-year-old, it was too much.

Before Vikram could say anything, the door burst open. A family of four stumbled in, clutching their chests, wheezing so hard it sounded like they were drowning in air. Vikram grabbed a jug and poured water into their hands, but he could see the truth in their faces – this was too late. One by one, their eyes went still.

'What's happened to them?' Suresh screamed, his voice breaking. 'Bhaiya, what's wrong with them? Why is this happening? Make it stop! Please make it stop!'

Vikram froze, his heart thudding in his ears. He had no answers. Only the terrible feeling that the nightmare was getting bigger, and there was no way out.

Then – WEEEOOOO! – a siren ripped through the night.

Angry voices muttered, 'Now they sound the alarm?'

Vikram's stomach dropped. His worst fear was real. Poisonous gas was pouring out from the Union Carbide plant.

5

WHEN THE DEAD FILLED THE STREETS

Sushma and Kanta jolted along in the back of the police van, the metal sides rattling with every bump. By the time they reached Bhopal, it was early morning and both girls were sore and grumpy. Their uncle led the entire Sharma clan into a police guest house in a quiet neighbourhood, high on a hill at the city's edge.

He pulled Mr Sharma aside and spoke in a low, urgent tone. Then, without even sitting down, he nodded to one of his constables. 'Stay with them,' he ordered, before hurrying back to whatever crisis was calling him.

As soon as their father came inside, Sushma said, 'Papa, what's happening? You aren't

saying a word. We haven't had any sleep. I am starving. Kanta and I are going to walk around the neighbourhood and find something to eat.'

Mr Sharma's eyes narrowed. 'Absolutely not. You're not to leave this compound. I can't talk about what's happening. Just stay here and you'll be safe.' The police orderly shook his head firmly, as if to underline the point.

'You never tell us anything and just expect me to obey you like a puppet,' screamed Sushma in frustration. 'I am tired and hungry, and I need to get out.'

'No, you don't,' her father screamed back and walked off. But Sushma had had enough. The moment Mr Sharma stepped away to talk to the rest of the family, Sushma made a face, grabbed Kanta's arm and whispered, 'Come on. They won't even notice we're gone.'

The girls lifted the heavy bar from the gate, slipped out and darted down a side road. The morning air was cool, and they picked their way downhill towards Bhopal's Upper Lake.

'Let's find some of that famous Bhopal poha,' Sushma grinned. 'And a cup of hot chai. We deserve it after that ride.'

A hulking shape came into view – a water buffalo, its massive head swinging side to side. Normally, they wouldn't have given it a second look, but this one stumbled, its legs wobbling under it. A deep, wheezy sound rattled in its throat.

'Come on, Kanta,' Sushma whispered. 'It's sick. Keep your distance.'

Kanta stepped wide around it, wrinkling her nose. 'I never knew Bhopal smelled so bad. It stinks!'

Sushma clamped a hand over her mouth and nose. 'Must be the lake,' she muttered. 'It's just vile.' The sisters giggled, trying to hold their breath, only to burst out laughing again. The smell, like boiled rotten cabbage, clung to them with every step.

After fifteen minutes, Sushma frowned. The streets were empty. Too empty. Even early in the morning, Indian city streets usually hummed with life – shops opening, tumblers of steaming tea in stalls, buses rumbling past.

They turned a corner and froze. A man lay face down in the street. Sushma hurried closer. 'He must be a beggar,' she whispered.

Kanta pointed silently. The man's mouth hung open, white foam clinging to his chin. His eyes – blood-red, bulging – stared at them, unblinking.

'Oh, Sushma, let's go back,' Kanta whimpered.

Before Sushma could answer, a door creaked open nearby. An old woman stumbled out, collapsing in front of them. Her eyes were just as red. White froth dribbled from her mouth.

Kanta shrieked and bolted. 'Kanta! Wait!' Sushma called, chasing after her. But in her pretty beaded chappals, she couldn't match her sister's speed. 'Slow down!' she gasped.

Her breath came in ragged bursts. Her legs

ached. Still, she pushed on – until they rounded another corner.

Bodies. The street was littered with them – some crawling weakly, most frighteningly still. Faces frozen in pain. Froth at their mouths.

Sushma caught Kanta by the arm. Her sister turned, eyes wide with terror. 'Sushmaaa!' she wailed.

Sushma pulled her close. Her heart was racing. She had never seen anything so scary in her life. A street full of dying people. She felt faint and wanted to throw up. What was happening? Why were all these people on the road, sick like this?

Then she saw her little sister's face. It was streaming wet with tears, and she was moaning.

Something inside Sushma shifted. She had, of course, always loved Kanta. But now, it was more than love – it was the absolute certainty that she had to protect her, no matter what. 'Come on. We have to leave.'

She gripped Kanta's hand tight and headed uphill. But the streets twisted and forked, and soon she realized she'd gone the wrong way. Her heart sank. *Why didn't I listen to Papa?*

Kanta started to cough, a deep, choking sound. Her eyes had become red. Panic surged in Sushma's chest. Was her sister getting sick too? She wanted to cry, but forced herself to stay calm.

'It's just a little further, baby,' she said, forcing a smile. 'We'll be safe soon. We just have to keep walking.' Her voice was steady, even if her legs felt like jelly. Somewhere up this hill, she told herself, was safety.

6

IN THE SAFE HOUSE

Sushma stopped and turned in a slow circle. Which way now? She'd never been to Bhopal before, but she knew the police guest house was near the lake. If she kept the lake behind her, picked a hill and climbed it, she might see it. If it wasn't the right hill, she could pick another.

It was a decent plan – until she chose the hill with the community centre.

Her legs throbbed. Kanta's little feet dragged, her coughs coming faster. Sushma's chest felt tight too, every breath shallow. Still, she kept up a steady stream of talk – about the wedding, about cousins, silly stories, even about ones

In the Safe House

Kanta had never met. Anything to keep her moving.

They were passing a low, dark building when a door swung open. A figure in the doorway waved frantically.

'Quickly!'

The voice cut through the fog in Sushma's head. She half-dragged Kanta through the gate and up the drive.

A boy about her age stood there, hair sticking up, eyes red with exhaustion.

'Inside, hurry! I'll shut the door. We have to keep it out.'

'Keep what out?' she asked, her heart thudding.

No answer. He yanked them inside, and bang! – the door slammed shut.

In seconds he was at a basin, splashing water into bowls, pushing wet cloths into their hands. A woman appeared beside him, showing them how to cover their noses and mouths.

Sushma took a breath through the damp cloth – easier. Only then did she realize how raw her throat felt.

'Where were you coming from?' the boy asked.

'Looking for food. Poha,' Sushma said.

He stared at her like she'd just suggested walking into a lion's cage.

'What?' she snapped. 'Why are you looking at me like that? What's happening? Why is everyone so sick? Tell me!'

Kanta started sobbing. Sushma pulled her close. 'It's okay. We're safe now. Safe,' she said, though her own pulse was hammering.

'You don't know?' His voice was sharp, then it softened. 'Poison gas leak. From the Union Carbide plant. People are dying.'

The words hit like stones. Before Sushma could speak, he went on, 'Stay with my little brother, Suresh. You can help by looking after him.'

The sisters told him about arriving from Delhi in the night, the train stopping outside Bhopal, the police van bringing them in.

He pointed through the window. 'That's the police guest house – on that hill. About thirty minutes' walk. But don't go now. The streets aren't safe.'

From across the room – cough! cough! cough! – an old man wheezed for air. The boy – Vikram – was gone in a heartbeat.

Moments later – thump, thump! – new arrivals stumbled in, coughing, eyes red, clutching their throats. Vikram met them at the door, splashing water over their faces, easing them to the wall, pressing cups of water into their hands. They smiled faintly, and that seemed to drive him harder – moving from one to the next, tying masks, washing eyes, never stopping.

One man's face shone with tears. Gas burns? Or grief? Sushma couldn't tell.

She looked around – pale faces, red eyes,

bodies curled on the floor with bundles for pillows. And everywhere, the low rasp of laboured breathing.

Kanta yawned. 'You're tired, aren't you?' Sushma asked.

'Yes,' Kanta and Suresh said together, holding out their arms. She picked up Kanta, rocking her with a lullaby.

'I'm tired too!' Suresh said hopefully.

She hugged him instead. He melted into her arms, his voice breaking. 'Vikram Bhaiya woke me in the night. I was angry – I wanted to sleep. But it was dark. People shouting. Dogs barking. I tied a wet dupatta over my face. He carried me on his shoulders and we ran. Sometimes we walked fast. I didn't know where we were going.'

'I wish I had a dupatta,' Kanta said. 'It smelled horrible. And no one carried me.'

'We saw a dog with puppies,' Suresh responded. 'They ... they were all dead. The

mother kept nudging them with her nose. They didn't move.'

Her voice shook. 'I was so scared.'

'Me too,' Suresh whispered. His eyes filled with tears. 'Two cows, staggering. Foam from their mouths. We had to run faster. My chin kept bumping Vikram Bhaiya's head. He didn't stop.'

'We also saw a buffalo,' Kanta said quietly.

'And then –' Suresh's voice dropped. 'People. So many people. Dead.'

'It's okay, you don't have to –' Sushma began.

'They were dead, dead, dead!' he cried. 'I don't want to die. I want my parents.' Sushma wrapped him in her arms until his sobs eased.

'Once we climbed the hill, no more dead people. The chowkidar let us in. He lives here alone. Vikram Bhaiya said we'd be safe from the gas.'

'I think he saved us,' Kanta whispered.

'Yes,' Suresh said. 'He saved us.'

Vikram passed by. Sushma caught his arm. 'I'm sorry. I was stupid.'

'There's nothing to forgive,' he said. 'Many didn't know. I grew up here ... and I love chemistry, so –' He shrugged.

But even he couldn't explain why the air below had turned into a killer that night.

7

STAY OR LEAVE?

'Bhaiyaaa ... I'm tired,' Suresh groaned. 'And bored.'

Kanta had climbed up beside him on the table. For hours, the two had been counting people. Every time someone came in, they'd yell out the new number like cricket commentators.

By now, the community centre was bursting – well over a hundred people. Many hadn't made it. Vikram had asked a few men to carry the bodies gently to a corner and cover their faces. The pile was growing.

'I'm coming, Suresh,' Vikram called over his shoulder. 'Just be patient!' He felt guilty that he had been neglecting his little brother.

But he had to help with the dead bodies. When he finally glanced back at the table where Suresh was, it was empty!

His heart skipped a beat. *Where—?!*

He ran frantically through the centre, looking for his brother and Kanta. Then he spotted them with Sushma by the sunny window. Kanta was in Sushma's arms, Suresh chattering away. He breathed a sigh of relief and steadied himself against the wall. He had not realized how tired he must be.

'... and the park has swings, and a slide and a big old banyan tree,' Suresh was saying. 'And when we're thirsty, Vikram Bhaiya buys us Frootis! I always ask for Thums Up, but he says –'

'Frooti is healthier,' Vikram finished with a grin, walking up to them.

Suresh made a face. 'Still ... Thums Up is better.'

Vikram ruffled his hair. 'Thanks for looking after them,' he told Sushma.

'Oh, we've been exploring your neighbourhood through the window,' she said. 'And I've learned you hand out Frootis as rewards.'

'Frootis!' both kids yelled.

Vikram laughed. 'Soon.'

'Bhaiya, when can we leave?' Suresh asked.

Vikram's smile faded. 'Soon, Suresh.' He wished his parents were with him. He shot a quick look at Sushma. These kids were seeing too much. But so were they.

It was morning now; the air was clearer. What Vikram didn't know was that the gas leak had stopped hours ago. Thirty tons had gushed out in minutes, then ten more over the next hour. The poisonous cloud crept low over the streets, heavy as a blanket.

He continued to keep the doors and windows shut. The chowkidar plopped down in front of the door like a guard dog.

The air inside had become stuffy. People fanned themselves. But no one wanted outside air. Some people wanted to head to hospitals. They didn't know the hospitals were already crammed – people lying in corridors, doctors just doing what Vikram was: keeping patients away from the gas, washing eyes and faces.

The community centre buzzed with argument – leave or stay?

'Oh, why did I leave the guest house?' Sushma muttered.

Kanta's eyes brimmed. 'How will Papa find us?'

Then – vroooom! – a police jeep screeched up. An officer strode in. The crowd surged towards him, shouting questions.

'Uncle!' Sushma cried, pushing through the crush. Kanta clung to her.

Their uncle scooped them into his arms. 'How did you get here? I've been looking everywhere!'

'I know,' Sushma mumbled. 'It's my fault. I was stupid.'

His arm tightened around her. 'I'll take you to your father.'

To the crowd, he said, 'It's safe to go out now. But don't go near the plant. Don't eat vegetables or fish from the lake. And ... be ready. The streets are bad – thousands dead.'

The chowkidar stepped forward. 'Sir, this boy saved us.'

'Yes, Vikram saved us!' voices chorused.

Vikram was pushed forward. 'Vikram Soni, sir,' he said, eyes lowered. 'I didn't do much. The doctor told me what to do ... then he died.' He pointed to the corner where over twenty bodies lay, covered.

The officer shook his hand. 'I'll put your name in my report.'

As the girls left with their uncle, Sushma hugged him. 'If you hadn't pulled us into the centre, we'd be gone,' she said with tears in her eyes. The four kids waved goodbye to each other.

Soon, the hall was empty. Vikram and Suresh were the last to leave.

'You should be a doctor,' the chowkidar said, his eyes shining. 'You saved so many people.'

Vikram smiled. 'I'm going to be a chemical engineer.'

The chowkidar grinned. 'Thank you, Doctor Sahib!' he called after them.

Vikram didn't turn around. He just kept walking into the thin morning light, carrying the weight of a night no one would ever forget.

8

HOSPITAL WITHOUT CURES

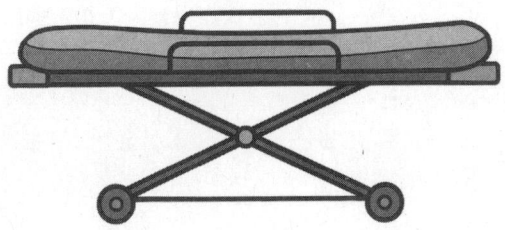

The ride back to the police guest house was awful.

Sushma recognized the streets. Just hours ago, she and Kanta had walked here, laughing about poha. Now –

Bodies. Everywhere.

In the middle of the road. Curled up on pavements. Faces frozen in pain.

'Don't look,' their uncle said, steering the jeep carefully. But it didn't matter. Even if she stared at the floor of the jeep, she could still see them in her mind.

The lanes were filled with people lying in strange, twisted positions. Kanta whimpered and buried her face in Sushma's chest.

Their uncle swerved around the dead. Bump-bump. Once, he had to stop completely. Thud. He climbed out and dragged three dead goats off the road.

Sushma's eyes darted to the sides of the street – buffaloes lying still, cows slumped where they'd been tethered, street dogs stretched out like they were sleeping. But they weren't.

She didn't cry. She didn't even feel like she could. She was ... numb.

The jeep pulled into the guest house compound. The girls leapt out before it even stopped properly.

'Papa!'

Footsteps. Shouts. And then – arms. Arms around them, squeezing so tightly it hurt. Sushma's tears, Papa's hands on their cheeks, Kanta sobbing into her father's shirt.

'I'm sorry, I'm sorry, I'm sorry,' Sushma kept repeating.

Her father didn't scold her. He didn't need to. He could see she already knew. Her shoulders shook with guilt. She'd already punished herself. He just held them close.

Then he stepped back, looking carefully at their faces. 'Your eyes,' he murmured. Bloodshot. Was it the gas? Or no sleep?

'Come,' he said. 'We're going to the hospital.'

The four of them bundled back into the jeep – Papa, their uncle and the two girls. As they drove towards Hospital Bhopal, the streets by the lake looked different – less devastation. No bodies lying in the middle of the road here.

But Sushma knew the truth. She had taken Kanta straight into the path of the gas. She clenched her fists in her lap. Never again. Never.

※

The hospital was worse than she could have imagined.

Hospital Without Cures

Crowds pressed at the gates, spilling into the parking lot, overflowing through the doors. The air was thick with noise – wails, shouts, coughs.

Sushma froze.

People lay on stretchers. On blankets on the ground. Not moving.

'They're ... dead,' she whispered.

Nurses rushed past, carrying bottles of water, rinsing eyes, dabbing faces with wet cloths.

'This is no different from what Vikram was doing!' Sushma burst out. 'Don't they have any medicine? This is a hospital!'

Her uncle grabbed a nurse by the arm. 'What is the treatment?'

The man shook his head. 'MIC. Methyl isocyanate. No one ... no one knows the cure.' He hurried off before they could ask more.

Sushma stared. People everywhere. And all the staff could do was wash their faces and help them breathe.

'We could have stayed with Vikram,' she muttered. 'It's the same care.'

Papa turned to her. 'Vikram?'

Sushma nodded. 'He saved us. He saved so many people.'

They tried to find somewhere to sit, but the hallways were jammed. People lay in rows on the grass outside, their eyes covered in thick cotton pads, giving the whole place an eerie, ghostly look. The smell of antiseptic mixed with something sour made Sushma feel dizzy.

She led her family to a bare patch of wall. 'Excuse me,' she said to two young men, 'can we sit here?' They shuffled aside, and Papa, Uncle and Kanta sat. Sushma crouched in front of them.

'Vikram just ... knew what to do,' she said. 'Before anyone else, he knew the gas was out. He pulled us in, washed our faces, gave us wet cloths. If he hadn't called to us, I don't know what would've happened.'

Her voice cracked. Papa pulled her into a bear hug. 'If you hadn't found him ... I don't know what I would have done either.'

Kanta wrapped her arms around Sushma's waist. 'Didi kept me safe,' she said fiercely.

Sushma trembled, then relaxed into their arms. Uncle hugged her too. 'Many would have given up,' he said. 'You didn't.'

Uncle touched their cheeks gently. 'I have to go,' he told them. 'The city ... it's bad. So many need help.'

After he left, Sushma told Papa everything – right from the moment she had snuck out of the gate. She made sure he knew it was her idea, not Kanta's. Papa's eyes widened in shock more than once, but by the end, he was quiet. He knew how lucky they'd been. How much they owed Vikram.

And he could see something else – Sushma had changed. She didn't need protecting. She had been thrown into the most frightening of

events and managed to get herself and her little sister to safety. Perhaps if he had told her more about the leak as they reached Bhopal, she wouldn't have bolted.

Papa decided then – he'd open up to her more. She would be able to help him look after Kanta too. He wondered why he hadn't seen it before.

9
A NEW FRIENDSHIP

The hospital was overflowing – people pressed against the gates, spilling into the street. No one could get proper treatment here.

Papa made the decision. 'We're walking back to the guest house.'

'I know the way,' he said, but now and then he glanced at Sushma. 'What do you think? This road or that one?'

Sushma's eyes swept the streets. 'That one,' she said, pointing. She tried to sound confident, but her stomach felt hollow.

They set off. The air was heavy and still. Twice they stepped around bodies in the road.

'Papa –' Sushma began.

'Keep moving,' he said tightly. 'We can't help them now.'

Sushma bit her lip. Kanta clung to her hand, walking fast to keep up. The streets felt eerie – too quiet except for the sound of their own footsteps. Tap-tap-tap.

Finally, there it was. The guest house gate. Clang! It shut behind them.

Sushma dropped into a chair. Her chest ached, and the tears came in a rush.

'Didi? Why are you crying?' Kanta asked, her voice small.

'I was so stupid,' Sushma whispered. 'I put you in danger. If anything had happened to you –' Her throat closed. 'Why did I leave the guest house?'

Kanta hugged her. 'It's okay, Didi.'

Papa crouched down, looking her in the eye. 'It's okay to cry. I'm proud of you.'

Sushma blinked. 'Proud? After what I did?'

'You took care of your sister,' Papa said. 'That matters.'

Knock-knock.

Kanta dashed to the door. 'Didi! It's Vikram!'

Sushma quickly wiped her face.

Vikram stood there, a little out of breath but smiling. 'See? I told you I knew where your guest house is.'

'But ... why did you come?' Sushma asked.

'I wanted to check you were safe. Both of you.' He shifted awkwardly, eyes on the floor.

'You're welcome here,' Sushma said with a grin. 'I've been telling Papa how you saved us.'

Vikram shook his head. 'You saved yourself. And ... thank you for helping Suresh. You kept him calm when I couldn't.'

Sushma's grin softened. 'He's a sweet kid.'

'Come meet my father,' she said.

Papa shook Vikram's hand warmly. 'Thank you, Vikram.'

They all sat as an orderly brought tea. Clink. Cups on the table.

Papa spoke first. 'I've been talking to doctors and officials. It was MIC – methyl isocyanate. Some say cyanide gas too. Union Carbide isn't confirming anything.'

'How many exposed?' Sushma asked.

Papa's mouth tightened. 'Over half a million people. Thousands are dead already. The rest ... many will suffer breathing problems, vision loss. Some may face cancer. And children yet to be born –' He stopped, looking at her. For a moment, he saw not his schoolgirl but someone listening steadily, taking all this in without flinching. He went on, a little more slowly.

'These are worst cases. We weren't in the worst-hit area. Let's hope for the best.'

Vikram leaned forward. 'Well ... there's one thing this night has made me realize. I really want to be a chemical engineer. Before, I wasn't sure – it sounded like it might be boring. But after seeing all this, it feels like I could be working on things that really matter.'

'Don't decide your future in a tragedy,' Papa said gently.

Kanta piped up, 'Be a doctor! The chowkidar said you'd be a good one.'

Vikram laughed. 'We'll see. But I think I've already made some good friends – not just here, but at home too.' He glanced at Sushma, then thought of Suresh, safe because of her, and smiled.

Outside, sirens wailed. Inside, the tea steamed quietly. For the first time since that terrible night, it felt like life might move forward – even if they would never forget what had happened.

The children promised to be friends forever. They exchanged phone numbers and promised to visit each other whenever they could. After tea, Vikram left for his house. The streets were clearer now, and Vikram hurried back to Suresh and his parents, who were back in Bhopal, safe and sound.

10

RECALLING THE TRAGEDY

Many years later, Vikram did not become a chemical engineer like he once thought. Instead, he became a doctor. His experience helping people in Bhopal changed the course of his life, changed him forever. And wherever he went, people asked him about that one night in particular – the night of the gas in Bhopal. They wanted to know what had happened, and what had happened afterwards.

Vikram would tell them:

Union Carbide was a big company. In 1969 it built a factory in Bhopal to make a powerful pesticide called Sevin. Farmers used it to protect their crops, and gardeners used it to protect flowers. The pesticide worked – but the chemicals inside it were very dangerous. The most dangerous one was called methyl isocyanate, or MIC. Even drops of water could make it explode into deadly gas.

At first, the factory imported MIC from America. Later, to save money, Union Carbide started making MIC right here in Bhopal. They stored it in three giant tanks under pressure. But the factory was old, and many of its safety systems didn't work anymore. Machines were broken. Alarms were silent. The company had cut staff, and the workers left on duty were not properly trained.

He would pause and shake his head.

'It was a recipe for disaster. And disaster came. MIC is not a poison you can see. It is a poison you can only smell at dangerous concentrations, but by then it may be too late. When it leaked, it killed everything – people, animals, fish, even birds in the sky. That night, thousands died. Some say 2,000, others say 3,000, maybe even 8,000. And the deaths didn't stop there. In the weeks and years after, many more died from breathing problems, cancer and sickness passed onto their children.'

Sushma grew up to become a journalist. As a witness to the tragedy and having an avid interest in the whole question of Union Carbide's responsibility for it, Sushma had put most of her time into uncovering the truth behind the tragedy. She remembers not only that night but also the years that followed.

Once, she had said, 'Before December 1984, the factory had already leaked gas several times. Workers had fallen sick. One had even died. But the company ignored the warnings. They cared more about money than about safety. Then came the night of the big leak – the worst industrial disaster in the world.

Recalling the Tragedy

'And after the gas came the court cases. Families who had lost loved ones wanted justice. More than a hundred lawsuits were filed against Union Carbide and its managers. But the company tried to escape responsibility. They argued, delayed and denied. After years of fighting, they were finally forced to pay compensation: $470 million. It sounded like a lot, but how can money replace a life? How can money heal the children who were never born, or the babies born sick?'

Her voice would soften.

'My younger sister, Kanta, can never have children. Was it the gas? We don't know. But I feel it in my heart. And no amount of money can fix that.'

WHY WE MUST REMEMBER

The Bhopal gas tragedy was one of the worst accidents the world has ever seen – and it happened in India.

It was terrible, but we must remember it. Children should learn about it in school. Families should tell the story at home. Because when we remember, we also learn. And when we learn, we make sure such a disaster never happens again.

OTHER BOOKS IN THE SERIES

26 January 2001, Chobari.

Seema was sipping tea. Her little sister, Padma, was playing with her dolls. Suddenly, the ground began to shake. At first, it was just a tremor. Then the floor rippled like waves. Walls cracked. Roofs collapsed. The sisters ran – but the world was falling apart.

Now they're trapped under the rubble, dust in their lungs, fear in their hearts. Seema knows she has to stay calm and find a way out before the next tremor hits. Can she save Padma and herself before it's too late?

26 December 2004, Mahabalipuram.

Arun Soni and his family are enjoying a holiday by the sea. But the fun doesn't last long. The very next morning, Arun notices something strange – the ocean has pulled back, leaving the beach bare. Before anyone can understand what's happening, a roaring wall of water comes crashing in.

A giant tsunami slams into the shore, smashing their hotel and flooding their room. In an instant, Arun is swept out to sea, fighting against the monstrous waves. Alone, terrified and far from safety, can Arun find his way back to his family?